ISBN: 9789491613067

MOUSE PRINTS PRESS
Prinsengracht 1053-S Boot
1017 JE Amsterdam Netherlands

Maurice's Valises

Moral Tails in an Immoral World

Book II: The Micetro of Moscow

By J.S. Friedman

Illustrations by Chris Beatrice

"Ninety-five?"

"Here."

"Ninety-six?"

"Here."

"Ninety-seven?"

"Here."

"And last, but not least, ninety-eight?"

"Here!"

"Haven't missed anyone, have I?"

"Nooooo," replied all ninety-eight grandmice.

"All here, Grandpa."

"Call me Maurice," said Grandpa. "Well, I suppose there's no point in my standing when I could be sitting."

And with that, he sat. But not just in any chair. He chose his absolute favorite, most comfortable ever, storytelling chair.

As always, it sat in his living room, deep in the woods, in the base of an old sycamore tree.

As always, at least in winter, a fire crackled in the fireplace.

As always, Maurice adjusted his snuggly storytelling scarf.

Winter's wind worried all the branches.

And the falling snow fell.

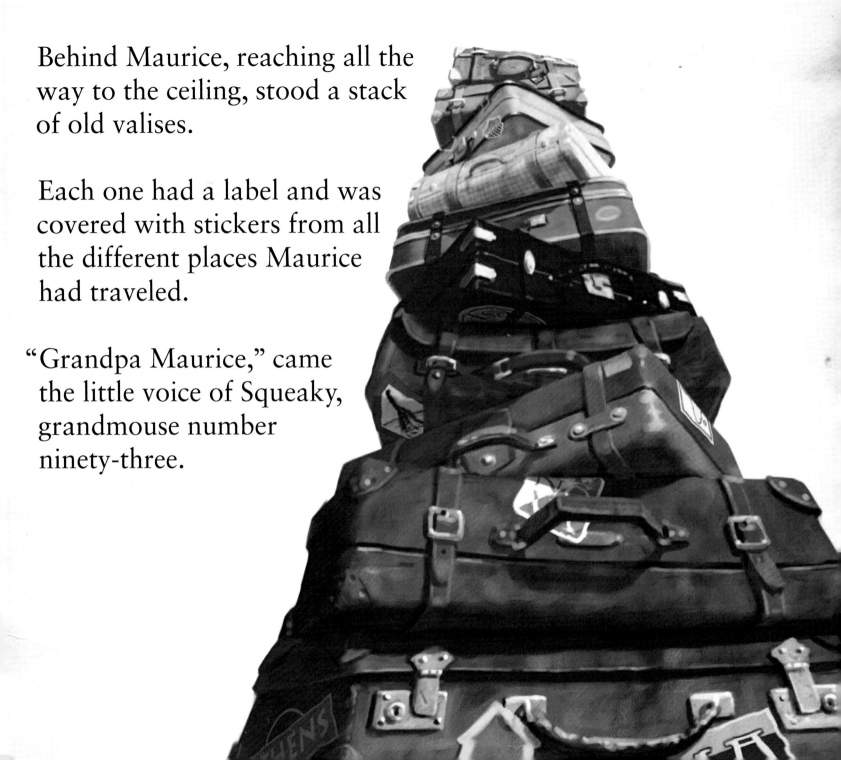

Behind Maurice, reaching all the way to the ceiling, stood a stack of old valises.

Each one had a label and was covered with stickers from all the different places Maurice had traveled.

"Grandpa Maurice," came the little voice of Squeaky, grandmouse number ninety-three.

"Tell your musical mouse story.
Tell us how you came to live in a desk drawer."

"Musical mouse? My, my," said Maurice,
rummaging through the stack of valises.

At last, he found the one he was
looking for.

He pulled it from the stack.

Undid the latch.

And peered inside.

Then, he sneezed a
mighty sneeze from all
the dust just waiting inside.

"Aaachooo!!!"

After recovering for a moment, he removed some old, well-worn sheet music, a Moral Scroll, and a funny fur hat.

On went the ushanka as he sat for a bit, quietly remembering. Then he cleared his throat and began.

PAW NOTES

A Moral Scroll is a paper with a wise saying written on it.
The saying is the lesson learned from a particular traveling tale.

A ushanka (also known as a shapka, or chapka) is a traditional Russian winter hat, which is extremely warm to handle the frigid Russian winters. It has earflaps, which can be folded up and tied at the top of the hat, or tied at the chin.

"Many years ago, I traveled on a barge full of mushrooms up a river called Moskva to Moscow."

"When we arrived, it was this very suitcase I had with me as I made my way to the old hotel by the river. When I got there, I could hear beautiful piano music coming from somewhere upstairs."

"I made my way past some old wooden mouse carts standing by the entrance and climbed the stairs to listen. But a heavy wooden door blocked my view.

I peeked under it.

There, I saw a man sitting at a piano, playing, and trying to write some music.

I saw a large wooden desk next to him.

And I saw a mouse's head pop out of the top drawer and disappear back under a sheet of music."

"After a while, the piano player closed the piano, got up, and came toward me. He opened the door and walked right past me.

This was my chance to meet the mouse.

So I ran across the floor, climbed up the desk, and dove into the drawer. I bumped right into the mouse, who was humming to himself as he felt around for his lost eyeglasses.

'Hello,' I said. 'I'm Maurice.'

'Hello,' said the mouse. 'I'm nearsighted–well, actually, I'm Henry. Welcome to my home.'"

"It turned out that Henry had spent years quietly living in the drawer.

Alone.

He had retreated to the attic because all the other hotel mice, that lived downstairs, made fun of him.

You see, he was little. The other mice weren't.

He had big ears. The other mice didn't.

He wore eyeglasses. They didn't.

And he loved music. They didn't."

"In short, he was short and he wasn't like them at all.

So, he contented himself spending each night in the attic, in the drawer, editing and adding to the music of the piano player.

As we talked, Henry told me how all the mice in the hotel depended on the food that came from the banquet hall below.

But this was a hard winter. Visitors were not coming to the hotel. There hadn't been many banquets. And food was running low."

"A lot of mice were packing to leave. Their carts (the ones I had passed on my way in) stood ready to go. Soon the hotel would be abandoned.

It turns out, the mice had been depending on the piano player to finish the music for a new ballet."

"A new ballet meant a kitchen full
of food for the premier.
And that meant no one
would go hungry.

Word was that the piano player was writing something about birds in a pond. (Truthfully, the mice didn't care if he wrote about frogs in an ocean—as long as people came and the kitchen was full.)

But there were still no signs of a banquet."

"The piano player—who Henry called Micetro, though he didn't look like a mouse—returned to his piano later that night.

He began playing, trying to write new music. Nothing worked.

After a while, he put his head down on the piano. Then, all of a sudden, he jumped up, threw the papers on the floor, and stormed out.

Henry sighed and snuck a peek over the edge of the drawer. Sheets of paper lay strewn across the floor.

He ran down to take a closer look at the papers, which were covered with black ink lines.

When Henry came back up he said, 'The Micetro is stuck again. But he is soooo close to finishing. Here, give me your help.'"

"With that, we lowered a pot of ink to the floor. Henry dunked his paws and his tail in the ink. Then, he walked back and forth on the paper, humming to himself, making even more lines.

Once he was finished, he turned and looked over his handiwork.

'There, maybe that will help,' he said. 'All the mice in this hotel are depending on him.'"

"The next morning, the downstairs mice began pulling their carts out of the hotel.

They didn't know how much Henry had helped the Micetro. Or that the Micetro was soooo close to finishing.

As soon as Henry realized the mice were leaving he ran down the stairs."

"'Wait, wait,' he cried. 'There will be a banquet, I just know there will. Please. Wait.'

But they didn't even look up to say the usual mean things to Henry. They were too sad and too hungry.

We climbed back up the stairs.

And there, to our delight, we found the Micetro hard at work, his hands skipping across the piano making the most magical music.

Happily, we made our way back to Henry's drawer and settled in to listen."

"Hour after hour, the Micetro worked. Adding a note here, a chord there, and an unexpected change in tempo.

Until suddenly, he sprang to his feet and yelled,

'I've finished! Finished!'

Then he practically pirouetted out into the cold night."

"Henry and I sat in the drawer without saying a single word.

We just looked at each other.

Then, I heard the voice of the Muse of Mice whisper, 'Maurice, believe in Henry and the Micetro.'

I looked at Henry, but he hadn't heard the Muse. And I could not explain what I heard. So we both went to bed hungry."

PAW NOTE

The Muse of Mice is the spiritual protector and guide of Maurice since birth.

"The next morning we woke to the bang and clang of carts on the street. Running to the nearest window, we looked down and saw workmen carrying baskets of food and flowers. Enough for a banquet! A banquet!

Henry and I looked at each other. Then, faster than you can say 'food,' we jumped from the drawer and ran to the street.

Workmen were hanging posters on lampposts announcing the premier of a new ballet to be performed: *Swan Lake*.

News of the banquet spread.

The mice were saved.

And every returning mouse greeted us with a smile and a 'Hooray Henry! Hooray for the musical mouse in the drawer! Hooray for the bird ballet!'"

"On the night of the premier, a steady stream of horse-drawn carriages arrived at the hotel. Each carried happy, laughing people.

The ballet had been brilliant!

Enchanting!

A success!

As the people feasted, the Micetro appeared. There wasa hush in the hall, then a thunder of applause as he bowed to everyone at the banquet.

The sounds echoed throughout the hotel. Upstairs in the attic, from his drawer, a well fed Henry took his little bow, too."

"From that evening on, every mouse, on every floor, knew they could count on the Micetro.

And, just as important, they knew they could count on Henry, the musical mouse in the drawer."

The End

There was a long silence. Then Squeaky spoke up.

"Grandpa Maurice, what is the lesson to be learned? What does the Moral Scroll say?"

Maurice slowly unrolled the scroll. Then he turned it around for all to see as he read it out loud:

Sometimes no matter how different you are from others, you are still special in your own, gifted way.

All the grandmice and their friends began to think about that.

But before they could ask Maurice any questions, his eyes began to close.

Just that fast, he began to snore.

It was a musical snore. And it sounded just a little like *Swan Lake*.

The end, again.
(*But more to come…*)

"We should say to each of them: Do you know what you are? You are a marvel. *You are unique*. In all the years that have passed, there has never been another child like you. Your legs, your arms, your clever fingers, the way you move. You may become a Shakespeare, a Michelangelo, a Beethoven. You have the capacity for anything.

If a man does not keep pace with his companions, perhaps it is because he hears a different drummer. Let him step to the music which he hears, however measured or far away."

– *Henry David Thoreau*

Henry David Thoreau was an American author, naturalist, pacifist, philosopher, and transcendentalist whose thinking has influenced generations around the world since his passing.

Acknowledgements

My special thanks to SolDesign for all their artistic input
and technical know-how in the creation of this book.
To Stephanie Arnold for her unwavering support and
crucial editorial contributions. To Joe Landry for his
Salzburg friendship and guidance. To my wife and family
for all their help. And to Chris Beatrice, for his illustrations
and vision and believing that Maurice is a special mouse.